GRODY'S
Not So GOLDEN RULES

Nicole Rubel

Silver Whistle
Harcourt, Inc.

San Diego   New York   London

Printed in Singapore

16 MAPLE ST.

My name is Grody. My parents say if you live by yourself on a distant planet, you can do whatever you like. My sister, Cookie, wishes I lived on Mars! But we live on Maple Street.

I've decided to make up some rules of my own.
I call them Grody's Golden Rules!

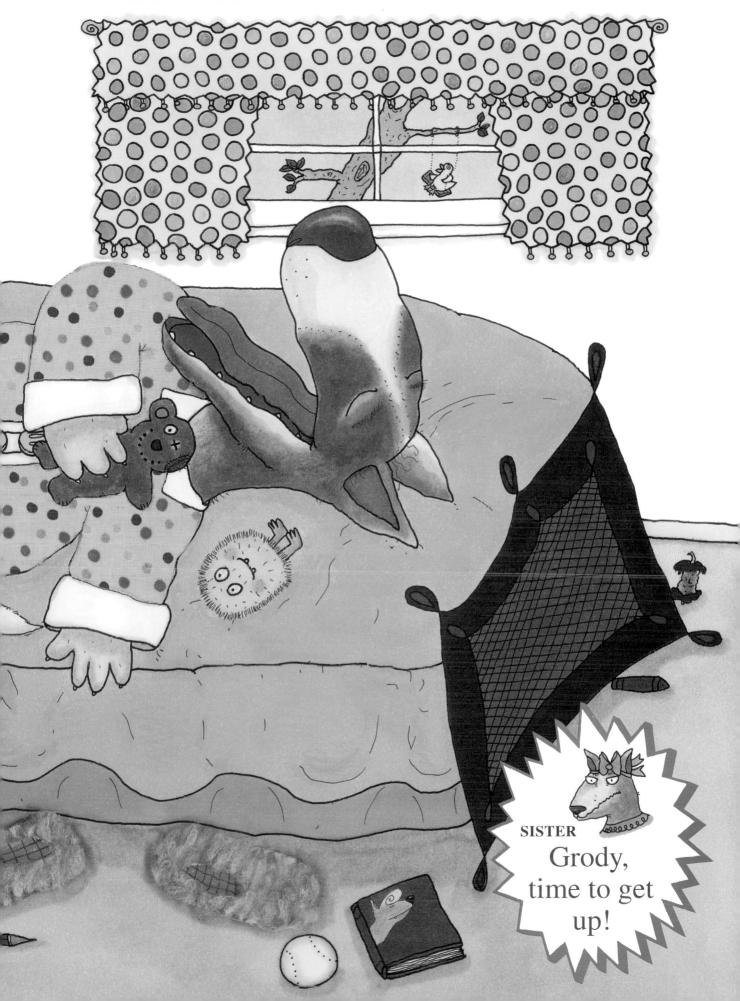

RULE NUMBER TWO
If you didn't follow Rule Number One, don't waste time brushing your teeth. They're just going to get dirty after breakfast!

RULE NUMBER THREE
Never clean your ears and you won't hear your mother calling you!

RULE NUMBER FOUR

Don't bother putting your clothes away. They will be easier to find if you leave them out!

RULE NUMBER FIVE

You'll have more room on the school bus if you don't change your socks for a month!

RULE NUMBER SIX
Always talk when your teacher is talking.
That way you get to leave the classroom.
You can always start over again next year!

RULE NUMBER SEVEN

In the school cafeteria, start with the good stuff in case you run out of time.

RULE NUMBER NINE
Always run down the
stairs instead of walking.
It saves time.

RULE NUMBER TEN

You'll drop less food on the table if you eat outside!

Why use a napkin when there's a perfectly good shirt to wipe your hands on?

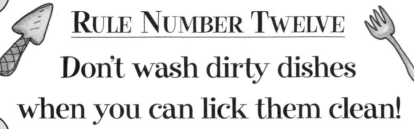

RULE NUMBER TWELVE

Don't wash dirty dishes
when you can lick them clean!

RULE NUMBER THIRTEEN

Why not stay up all night watching TV? You're just going to have to get up again in the morning!

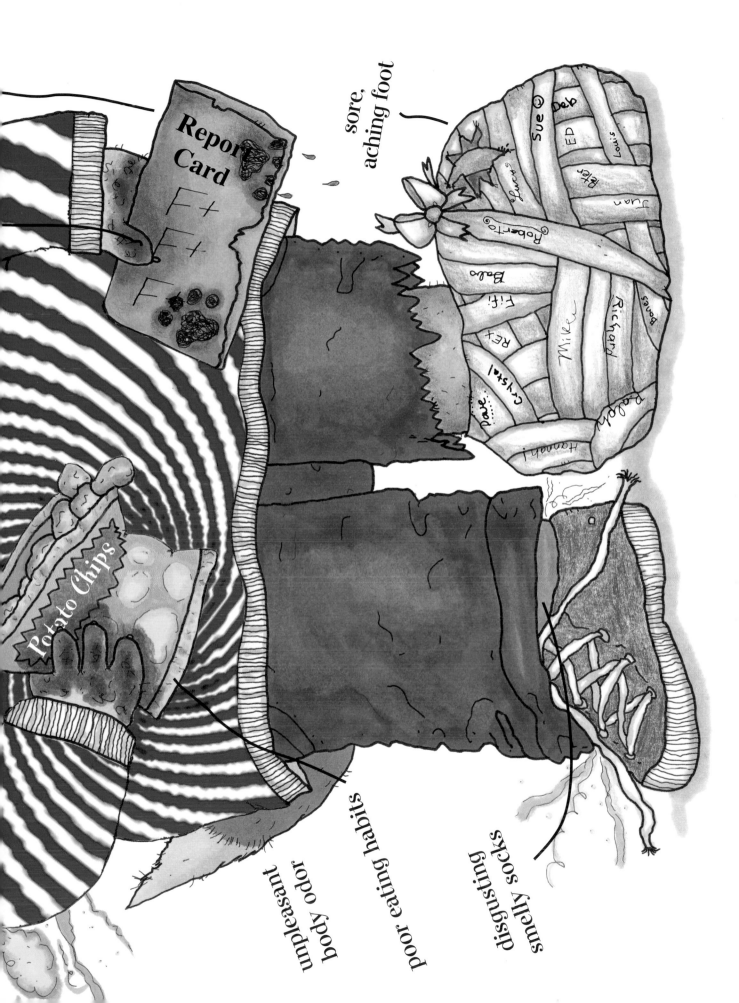

I wish to thank my parents, who inspired me to create this book
—N. R.

Library of Congress Cataloging-in-Publication Data
Rubel, Nicole.
Grody's not so golden rules/Nicole Rubel.
p.   cm.
"Silver Whistle."
Summary: Unhappy with how adults tell him to behave,
Grody makes up his own self-centered rules.
[1. Dogs—Fiction.   2. Behavior—Fiction.]   I. Title.
PZ7.R828Gr   2003
[E]—dc21   2001005654
ISBN 0-15-216241-0

First edition

A C E G H F D B

The artwork in this book was done on
marker paper with black ink, markers,
colored pencils, watercolor, fabric,
fabric paint, and photographs.
The display type was set in Bostonia.
The text type was set in Elroy and Times.
Color separations by Bright Arts Ltd.,
Hong Kong
Printed and bound by Tien Wah Press,
Singapore
This book was printed on totally chlorine-free
Enso Stora Matte paper.
Production supervision by Sandra Grebenar
and Pascha Gerlinger
Designed by Suzanne Fridley